The Creepy Thing

BY FERNANDO KRAHN

CLARION BOOKS
TICKNOR & FIELDS : A HOUGHTON MIFFLIN COMPANY
NEW YORK

Clarion Books
Ticknor & Fields, a Houghton Mifflin Company
Copyright © 1982 by Fernando Krahn

Printed in the United States of America

Library of Congress Cataloging in Publication Data

Krahn, Fernando.   The creepy thing.
Summary: A small boy goes fishing and catches
a creepy thing with a strange life of its own.
[1. Stories without words]   I. Title.
PZ7.K8585CR   [E]   81-18148
ISBN 0-89919-099-5   AACR2